MOLLY'S FIRST FESTIVAL

Written and Illustrated
by Katherine O'Shea

Mum

Dad

Ted

Molly

It was Molly's first trip to a festival,
Would they love it? She just didn't know.

This book has been made possible though the power of crowdfunding.
A massive thanks to the following people for their contributions:

KICKSTARTER

Liam O'Shea – Zofia Coulton – Sue Hessom – Naidre Werner – Kirsty Kelly – Deborah Parkes
Daisy Fitzsimmons – Dennis – Victoria Thorpe – Keeley, Pete, Em & Sully (Vibes Life Us) – Lyn Lewis
Steve Reynalds – Bigi Luetchford – Candice Kent – Emma Foley – Gail Wallbank – Andy and Holly Coulton-Wood
Anna "Granna" Whelan – Rebecca McCarter – Ellie Cook – Everette Taylor – Sophie Intiglietta – Maureen Houghton
William Law – James O'Shea – Fred Weston – The Pestel family – Gaile – Indiana Mai Peers – Maya Middlemiss
Jude - Polly Walker – Jo Beaumont – Annabel Smyth – Niovi – Simon Cook – Elsie, Chris and Stanley Kinlock
Joanna Coulton – Jenny Coulton – Amanda Nicholls – Emily Scoggins – Rosemarie Shaw – Sarah Slater
Annie Taylor Laxa – Caroline Dixon – Clare Stafford – Lindsey Duckett – Hattie Mitchell – Teresa Harmand
Jasmine Moulden – Julie Robertson – Anne Gardner Thorpe – Keira Forrest – James Thomas – Esme
Jennie Thomas – Claire Wallbank – Jim O'Shea – Abby – Jayde Elliott – Marcie – Tina Uren – Mary – Ruby Jones
Paul Channon – Shelley Winter – Lucy Hawkins – Lucy Tyler – Jennifer Doherty – Claire Benn – Bun Mitchell
Christina Rose Brown – Owen Wallbank – Dave Parkes – Vanessa Staunton – Rachel Bone – Lynsey Rawbone
Leanne Guest – Gemma Trickey – Antony Lorman – Natalie Burton – Rachael Lorman – Oskar Lorman – Hanna Smith
Catherine Lawson – Tim Coulton – Philip Eliot – Liz Clemmow – (Memory of) Anne-Marie Dansicker
Rosie McLaughlin – Lauren Jones – Riley Erin Kinzie (Big Feelings Books) – Isaac O'Neil – Penny Sexton

I would also like to thank the following small businesses:
Raising Ravers children's fashion - whose Rainbow Boogie bomber jacket can be found on page eight - *raisingravers.com*
The Ilex Wood skincare - who are selling their all-natural beauty products on page ten - *theilexwood.com*
Fabulous Lemon Drops family entertainers - who are playing onstage on page thirteen - *fabulouslemondrops.com*

Dedicated to my Auntie Barbara,
she was a true festival spirit.

Words and Illustrations by Katherine O'Shea.
Design/layout by Katherine O'Shea.
With special thanks to Jennifer Doherty for editing.

"I'm so excited! Can we go every year?"

And Mum said, "Let's see how we go..."

They had torches,
and sun cream,
and wellies,
and socks...

It seemed to just go on and on.

But finally, with the car stuffed to the roof,
And a "BEEP" of their horn - they were gone!

Oh, will it be sunny? Or miserable?
Who knows what to expect at a festival?

When they got to the site they
joined a huge crowd,

Carrying tents and
camp chairs and mats.

Everyone was super-sparkly and bright,
And wearing ridiculous hats.

In the morning they went to the big Main Stage,
It looked just like it did on the telly!

There were so many people! And colours! And flags!
It was loud ....and a little bit smelly.

People were singing and dancing around,

There was mess all over the place.

"Uh, oh!" said Ted. But a man with a stick said,
"Don't worry - we'll Leave No Trace."

Oh, isn't it crazy? And so colourful?
Anything can happen at a festival.

The next day they saw a Very Loud Man,
Who kept jumping and shaking his head.

Molly went to the Kids' Zone with Dad and with Ted,
Where they met a celebrity!

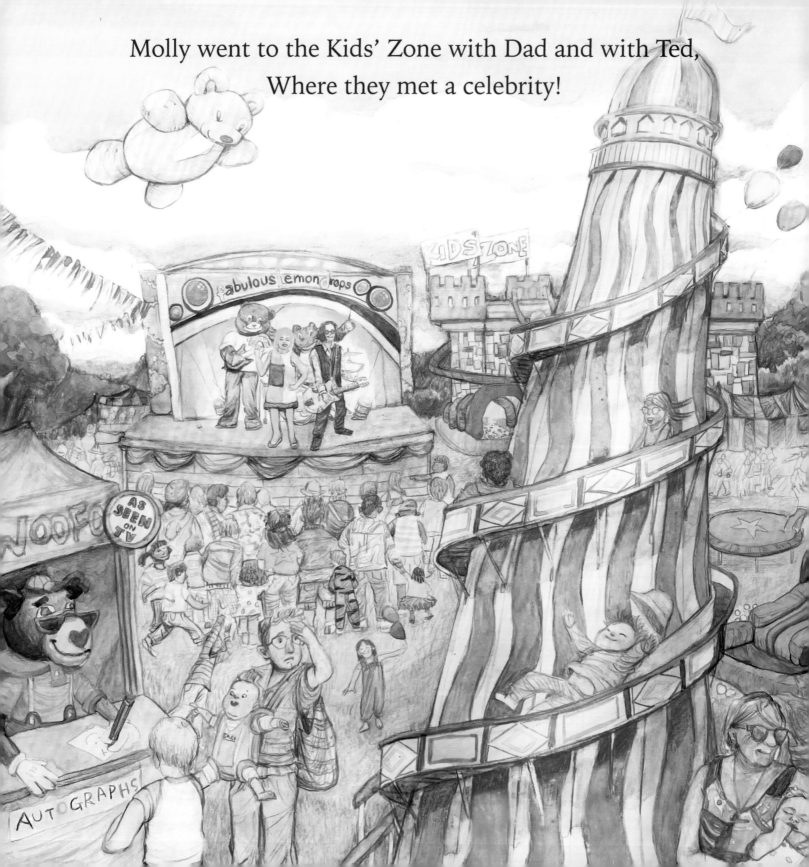

They met up with Mum at the Chill Out tent,
And tried some spicy chai tea.

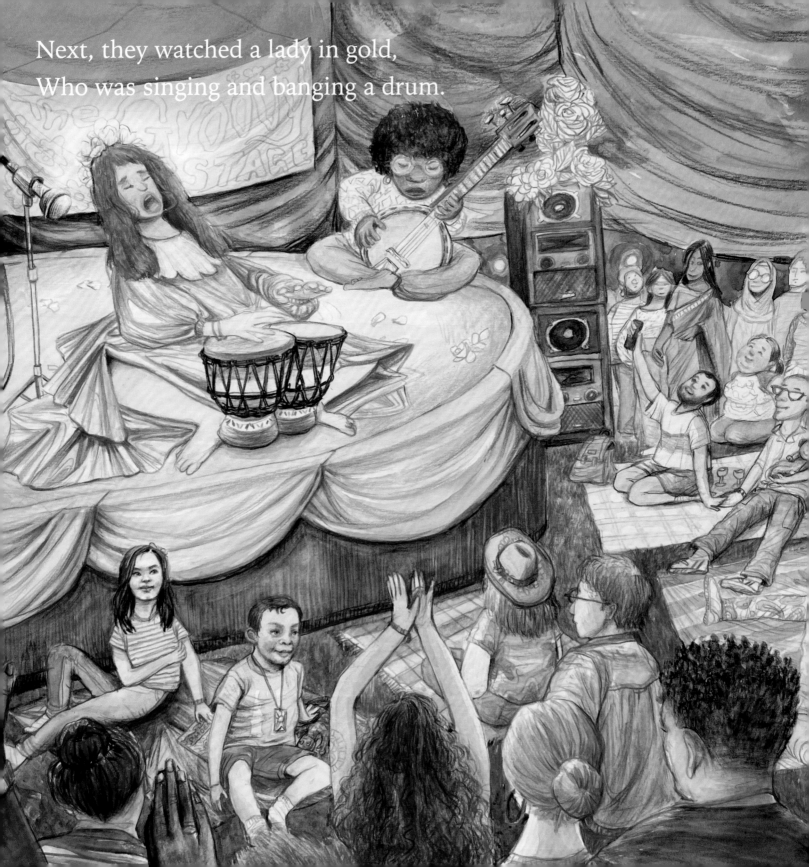

Next, they watched a lady in gold,
Who was singing and banging a drum.

Oh, what a noise! Oh, what a big mess!
At a festival, who knows what comes next?

By Sunday they were all a bit tired and mucky,
And getting quite grumpy and cross.

Molly's unicorn toy got dropped in the mud,
And Ted wanted candy floss.

They were queueing for food at a burger van,
"This is taking forever!" Mum said.

"COME ON!!!!"

wailed Dad, who looked like he'd rather be anywhere else instead.

But - the weirdest thing Molly had ever seen, Was wobbling up to the van...

A llama
on stilts
came up
to Dad,
And told him,
"Peace out, Man!"

First Mum started to laugh.
Then Dad did too.
Then Molly,
then Ted,
and the burger van crew.

You have to admit
it's hard to frown,
When you're wearing
a rainbow flower crown.

For the rest of the day they had so much fun,
They disco-danced for hours.

They saw a big tree made of recycled bottles,
And learnt how to make paper flowers.

At the end of the day when the sun was setting,
And the lights were beginning to glow,

They walked up the hill to the festival sign,
With the fields all twinkling below.

"Festivals are magic," Molly said, with a yawn,
As she lay down to snooze on the hill.

Quietly, Mum and Dad looked at each other,
And decided they thought so as well.

Oh, wasn't it lovely? There was nothing to fear,
Of course, we'll be coming back next year!

THE END